# CAT, MOUSE

TAHIR SHAH

ANNITA LUXON

# CAT, MOUSE

*A Teaching Story*

TAHIR SHAH

ANNITA LUXON

MMXXIV

Secretum Mundi Publishing Ltd
124 City Road
London
EC1V 2NX
United Kingdom

www.secretum-mundi.com
info@secretum-mundi.com

First published by Secretum Mundi Publishing Ltd, 2024
A version of this story originally appeared in *Scorpion Soup* by Tahir Shah, 2013

CAT, MOUSE



Artwork drawn by Annita Luxon



A CIP catalogue record for this title is available from the British Library.

ISBN 978-1-915876-01-0

VERSION 18072023

Visit the author's website:
Tahirshah.com

The greatest dreams come true beyond the far horizon.

*Egyptian saying*

# Teaching Stories

When I was small, I was told stories from morning till night.

I was told stories about genies and witches and about great birds that could carry away elephants on their wings… and stories about distant kingdoms and magical lands ruled by warrior kings.

I was told stories of good and bad… stories of hope and others of despair.

I was even told stories about stories.

And all the while, I listened, amazed.

The more I listened, the more my mind worked… and the more I came to understand that these stories had a power about them, a secret lifeblood all of their own.

They were magical instruments, machineries that could alter states of mind and change the way we think.

But most importantly of all, stories can teach us, without us realizing that they are doing so at all.

Part of the default programming of man, stories are within us all.

Born into us, they make us who we are – they make us human.

Since earliest childhood, I have feasted on stories as a way of learning about the world, and learning about myself. They have been my dictionary and my encyclopaedia, my classroom, my guide, and my very best friend.

To descend down through the layers of stories is to be reborn, into a dominion of fantasy – one touched by real magic.

Pre-eminent within the great treasuries of tales, it is teaching stories like this one that have shown me the path to follow beyond the next horizon, and have made me the man I am.

Tahir Shah

There was once an island
on which cats reigned supreme.

They lived like royalty, gorging themselves on the abundant mouse populace, forcing those mice that were not devoured to work for them as slaves.

In the factories and in the mines, the mice laboured from before dawn to well after dusk.

All the while, their cat masters became increasingly cruel – and lazier and lazier – as the mice served them.

From time to time a lone mouse would escape his shackles, jump up, and taunt the cats.

Such breakouts always ended the same way.

The offending mouse would be caught, tortured, and slowly devoured while still alive.

Rather than become disheartened at their fate,
the mice became increasingly tolerant.

As the months and years dragged on, the mice slaves found that they could endure worse and worse conditions.

And, as they did so, their feline masters became progressively neglectful.

Eventually, the day came when every single cat fell asleep during the long, hot summer afternoon.

Seizing the moment, the mice in the slave camp managed to unfasten their chains and break free.

Having tied up the cat guards,
they stormed the pleasure domes in
which their feline masters reclined.

Strengthened by years of servitude,
the mice quickly gained the upper hand.

The cats had no choice but to become slaves to the mice.

Begrudgingly, they did so.

But, so hardened by their own experience as slaves, the mice were themselves ruthless masters.

Regarding the cats as vermin, they thought nothing of executing them summarily for even the most trifling misdemeanour.

The cat numbers fell dramatically.

Indeed, such was the mouse rage that
the cats were almost entirely wiped out.

Their numbers reduced to a handful,
the survivors plucked up their courage
and broke free.

Making their way by night to the beach,
the last surviving cats built a raft with a flimsy
mast and sail, and they took to the sea.

Within a day or two, all but one had expired.

A scrawny tabby cat, he survived because his treatment as a slave to the mice had been especially harsh.

As a result, he had learned to harness reserves of strength that other cats never realized they possessed.

After days and nights on the waves, this last bedraggled cat reached another island – an island ruled over by ghouls.

Fearsome in looks and demeanour, the ghouls had a legend that one day, a saviour unlike them would come from beyond the distant horizon and rule over them.

Every ghoul child was raised with the legend and could quote it by heart.

Each morning and night, all the ghouls clustered together on the sands and peered out to where the water met the sky.

Centuries had passed,
and no saviour ever came.

But still they waited.

And they never gave up hope.

Searching the horizon for their saviour became important in itself – a kind of divine act by which the ghouls lived.

Twice daily they gathered together as
a community to keep the society strong.

And in this a way, the traditions and folklore were passed from one ghoul generation to the next.

On the evening of the cat's arrival at the island, the ghouls were clustered down at the beach, singing a song venerating their saviour – the saviour who had not yet come.

Some of them had forgotten why
exactly they met there twice daily.

Yet in many ways it didn't seem to matter why they were there, so much as the fact that they were.

One evening, a ghoul child suddenly pointed towards the darkened swell.

‘Look there!’ he cried. ‘Look there!’

'Keep singing and stop making a noise,'
snarled one of the ghoul elders.

'Father, look!'
exclaimed another of the children.

A surge of anticipation swept through the group, as all the ghouls – young and old – set eyes on the raft.

The cat was pulled to safety and at once was taken to the house that had been built for the saviour, were he ever to come.

Fed delicious morsels of fish, he was fanned with palm fronds and told repeatedly how very special he was.

Unable to believe his luck, the cat
enjoyed the indulgence for a long while.

He learned to speak the ghoul language and became well versed in the ghoulish lore and tradition, of which he himself was a central part.

But now that their saviour had arrived,
the ghouls' society began to collapse.

With no reason to cluster down at the beach,
the community became fragmented.

The legends and the songs were forgotten.

And then, eventually, the ghouls began to question why they had to support such a lazy tabby cat, even though he was supposedly their saviour.

Fortunately, one of the ghouls was more enlightened than the others and understood exactly what was happening.

Little did he know that it was his own ancestor who had devised the idea of the saviour arriving as a device to keep the community in harmony.

Taking ink and paper, he wrote a manuscript entitled *Wisdom for Ghouls and Cats*.

The document was a handbook
to life and to values.

Suffocating the cat while he slept, the ghoul left the manuscript beside the bloated body.

When they found the remains of their saviour,
the ghouls were disconsolate.

They jumped up and down,
and beat themselves with sticks.

‘What will we do now that our saviour has left us?’ they cried as one.

The enlightened ghoul jabbed
a hand towards the document.

‘The saviour may have gone to new hunting grounds,’ he said, ‘but he has left us this.’

‘It will become the core of our new faith!’
cried the ghouls.

From that day forwards, the ghouls drew answers to all their problems from the manuscript which, with time, was regarded as well beyond sacred…

… a bible of its own, known simply as …

*… Wisdom for Foolish Ghouls and Beloved Cats.*

*Finis*

*About the Author*

Descended from a long line of storytellers, writers, and savants, Tahir Shah is one of the most prolific authors of his generation. He has published more than sixty books in numerous genres, including travel, fiction, and fantasy, as well as tales for children.

Raised in the tradition of Eastern 'teaching stories', Shah is passionate about stories and storytelling. He regards the ability to learn from folklore as being in us all, what he calls a 'default setting of humankind'. As well as having written scores of books, Shah has made documentaries for National Geographic TV and The History Channel. He is the founder and CEO of the charity, The Scheherazade Foundation.

*About the Artist*

Annita Luxon is a professional self-taught artist based in Thessaloniki, Greece. She draws inspiration from poetry and literature, having a soft spot for H.P. Lovecraft, Edgar Allan Poe, Charles Baudelaire, Dante Alighieri, and cats. The mediums of work are traditional oil paints and dip-pen and ink. She has participated in a number of fantasy and comic conventions and her works have been on display in art galleries and featured in magazines around the world.

*Books By Tahir Shah*

*The Writer's Craft*

The Reason to Write

Workbook: Comprehensive, Volume I & II

Workbook: Fantasy, Volume I & II

Workbook: Fiction, Volume I & II

Workbook: Historical Fiction, Volume I & II

Workbook: Teaching Stories, Volume I & II

Workbook: Travel, Volume I & II

*Novels*

Jinn Hunter: Book One – The Prism

Jinn Hunter: Book Two – The Jinnslayer

Jinn Hunter: Book Three – The Perplexity

Hannibal Fogg and the Supreme Secret of Man

Casablanca Blues

Eye Spy

Godman

Paris Syndrome

Timbuctoo

Midas

Zigzagzone

*Nasrudin*

Travels With Nasrudin

The Misadventures of the Mystifying Nasrudin

The Peregrinations of the Perplexing Nasrudin

The Voyages and Vicissitudes of Nasrudin

Nasrudin in the Land of Fools

*Travel*

Trail of Feathers

Travels With Myself

Beyond the Devil's Teeth

In Search of King Solomon's Mines

House of the Tiger King

In Arabian Nights

The Caliph's House

Sorcerer's Apprentice

Journey Through Namibia

*Teaching Stories*

The Arabian Nights Adventures

Scorpion Soup

Tales Told to a Melon

The Afghan Notebook

Daydreams of an Octopus & Other Stories

The Caravanserai Stories

Ghoul Brothers

Hourglass

Imaginist

Jinn's Treasure

Jinnlore

Mellified Man

Skeleton Island

Wellspring

When the Sun Forgot to Rise

Outrunning the Reaper

The Cap of Invisibility

On Backgammon Time

The Wondrous Seed

The Paradise Tree
Mouse House
The Hoopoe's Flight
The Old Wind
A Treasury of Tales
The Tale of Double Six
The Forgotten Game
King of the Jinns
The Destiny Ring
Changing the World
Cat, Mouse
Frogland
Mittle-Mittle
Capilongo
The Princess of Zilzilam
The Singing Serpents
The Tale of the Rusty Nail
The Unicorn's Tear
The Clockmaker Who Travelled Through Time
The Fish's Dream
The Man Whose Arms Grew Branches
The Most Foolish of Men
The Shop That Sold Truth
Qwerty
Renaissance
The Man With the Tiger's Head
The Kingdom of Blink
The Wisdom of Celestine
Dream Soup
The Skeleton Factory
An Unexpected Gift

The Problem Exchange
The Pharaoh Code
The Monkey Puzzle Club
Liquid Time
Cat Dog, Dog Cat
Princess Pickle's Laugh

*Anthologies*

The Anthologies: Africa
The Anthologies: Ceremony
The Anthologies: Childhood
The Anthologies: City
The Anthologies: Danger
The Anthologies: East
The Anthologies: Expedition
The Anthologies: Frontier
The Anthologies: Hinterland
The Anthologies: India
The Anthologies: Jinns
The Anthologies: Jungle
The Anthologies: Magic
The Anthologies: Morocco
The Anthologies: Nasrudin
The Anthologies: People
The Anthologies: Quest
The Anthologies: South
The Anthologies: Taboo
The Anthologies: Teaching Stories
The Clockmaker's Box
The Tahir Shah Fiction Reader
The Tahir Shah Travel Reader

*Research*

Cultural Research

The Middle East Bedside Book

Three Essays

*Edited by*

Congress With a Crocodile

A Son of a Son, Volume I

A Son of a Son, Volume II

*Screenplays*

Casablanca Blues: The Screenplay

Timbuctoo: The Screenplay

## A REQUEST

If you enjoyed this book, please review it on your favourite online retailer or review website.

**Reviews are an author's best friend.**

To stay in touch with Tahir Shah, and to hear about his upcoming releases before anyone else, please sign up for his mailing list:

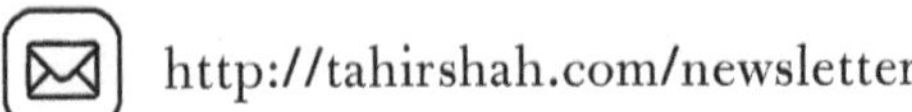

http://tahirshah.com/newsletter

And to follow him on social media, please go to any of the following links:

http://www.twitter.com/humanstew

@tahirshah999

http://www.facebook.com/TahirShahAuthor

http://www.youtube.com/user/tahirshah999

http://www.pinterest.com/tahirshah

https://www.goodreads.com/tahirshahauthor

**http://www.tahirshah.com**

www.ingramcontent.com/pod-product-compliance
Lightning Source LLC
Chambersburg PA
CBHW030523310726
48979CB00010B/1779/J

* 9 7 8 1 9 1 5 8 7 6 0 1 0 *